Go! G

written by Pam Holden

A train is going past.

인삼녹용-디
대

A bus is going past.

SCHOOL BUS
EMERGENCY DOOR
STOP

A boat is going past.

A car is going past.

A plane is going past.

A bike is going past.

A truck is going past.

A helicopter is going past. Go!